For Dad–
RC

SIMON AND SCHUSTER

First published in Great Britain in 2007 by Simon & Schuster UK Ltd

Africa House, 64-78 Kingsway, London WC2B 6AH

A CBS COMPANY

Text and illustrations copyright © 2007 Ross Collins

The right of Ross Collins to be identified as the author

and illustrator of this work has been asserted by him in accordance

with the Copyright, Designs and Patents Act, 1988

Book designed by Genevieve Webster

The text for this book is set in Happy

The illustrations are rendered in watercolour

A CIP catalogue record for this book is available from

the British Library upon request

ISBN 1 416 91669 5

EAN 9781416916697

Printed in Singapore

1 3 5 7 9 10 8 6 4 2

My Amazing Dad

Ross Collins

SIMON AND SCHUSTER
London New York Sydney

Snip and Max were playing
a game of Leap-Croc, when suddenly . . .

Whoosh!

"What was **that?**" gasped Snip.

"That," smiled Max proudly, "was **my dad.**
I'm going to be just like him when I grow up."

"What does your dad do, Snip?" asked Max.

"I don't really know," said Snip. "He goes away in the morning and comes back at night . . . but everything in between is a mystery."

Up ahead they spotted Stripe.

"What does your dad do, Stripe?" Snip asked.
"My dad's the best at hiding," grinned Stripe.
"I'm going to be just like him when I grow up."

Snip frowned. "I'm not sure if my dad is any good at hiding."

A bit later, they ran into Trunkle.

"Hey, Trunkle," said Max. "What does your dad do?'

"My dad can spray water higher than the tallest trees," gushed Trunkle. "I'm going to be just like him when I grow up."

Snip fretted. "I don't know if my dad could even blow bubbles!"

Next they bumped into Beaky and Spot.
    "What's going on?" asked Snip.

    "Our dads are having a race to see who's faster,"
giggled Beaky, flapping her wings with excitement.

    "We're going to be just like them when we grow up,"
smiled Spot.

    "Can your dad run fast, Snip?" asked Beaky.

    "I don't think so," said Snip. "His legs are kind of . . ."
                    "Stubby?" suggested Max helpfully.

As they headed back into the trees,
they heard a great booming noise.

Bongo rolled out of the bushes.

"That's my dad," said Bongo proudly.
"He beats his chest louder than anyone.
I'm going to be just like him when I grow up."

"Does your dad have a chest, Snip?" asked Max.
"Well . . . he's got a belly," mumbled Snip.

Down by the river, they ran into Wallow.

"Hi, Wallow," sighed Snip. "I guess
your dad does something really amazing, too."
"Well," said Wallow, "he can stay
underwater for ages without ever coming up for air . . .
I'm going to be just like him when I grow up."
"Wow!" gasped Max.

"I knew it," groaned Snip, as they trudged back home. "Everyone has a cooler dad than me."

"Chin up, Snippo!" chirped Max. "I'm sure your dad does *something*."

But Snip wasn't so sure.

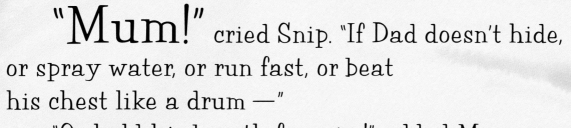

"Mum!" cried Snip. "If Dad doesn't hide, or spray water, or run fast, or beat his chest like a drum —"

"Or hold his breath for ages!" added Max.

"Or hold his breath for ages, then **what does he do all day long?**"

Mum smiled her big toothy smile and wrapped her tail around Snip like she used to do when he was just an egg.

"Come with me," she said. So they walked downstream until they reached the high reeds.

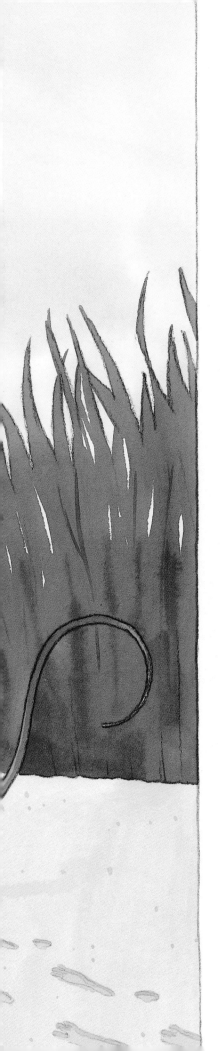

Slowly and quietly, Snip's mum
parted the grass for Snip to see.
"What's Dad doing?" asked Snip.

"Your dad," explained Mum,
"is the one who teaches everyone how to hide,
and run fast, and do all those special things
they'll do when they grow up."
"Wow, Snip!" said Max.
"Your dad is kind of . . ."

"Amazing!" shouted Snip, giving his dad a giant crocodile hug.

"Dad?" asked Snip, beaming proudly.
"Will you teach me how to do all that stuff too?

His dad smiled.
    "Sure, son. Let's start with some fishing."

"Hey, Dad," said Snip
as they headed upriver.
  "I want to be just like you when I grow up!"

M
O
U
N
T
A
I
N
S

Stripes
grazing place

Spot and Beaky's
running place

PLAINS

Trunkle's
water hole

Bongo's
bit

JU